P9-DFT-141

Creative Director: Susie Garland Rice

The Velveteen Rabbit

Adapted by Ashley Crownover
Illustrated by Sherry Neidigh

Dalmatian Press

There was once a beautiful Velveteen Rabbit. His coat was spotted brown and white and his ears were lined with pink satin. On Christmas morning he was the best thing in the Boy's stocking. For at least two hours the Boy loved him, then in the excitement of looking at all the new presents the Velveteen Rabbit was forgotten.

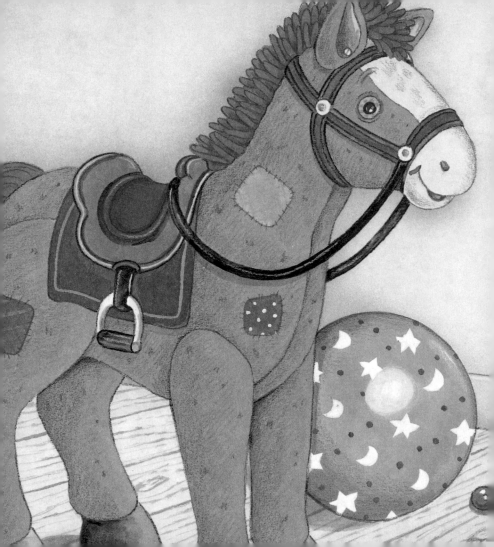

For a long time nobody paid much attention to the Rabbit. The mechanical toys were rude to him because he was only a stuffed bunny. But the Skin Horse, who had been there longer than any of the other toys and knew all about toy magic, was very kind.

"What is Real?" the Rabbit asked the Skin Horse one day.
"Does it mean having batteries or lights?"
"Real isn't how you are made," said the Skin Horse. "It's
a thing that happens to you. When a child loves you, then
you become Real."

One evening at bedtime, the Boy couldn't find the china dog that slept with him, so his mother gave him the Rabbit instead. From then on the Velveteen Rabbit slept in the Boy's bed every night. The Boy made tunnels for him in the bedcovers, and the Rabbit slept snug and warm in the Boy's arms.

Spring came, and wherever the Boy went, the Rabbit went, too. He had rides in the wheelbarrow and picnics on the grass. One day, he heard the Boy tell his mother, "He's a Real Rabbit, not a stuffed toy." That was the happiest day of the Rabbit's life.

After a while, the Velveteen Rabbit got raggedy
from being loved so much. Some of his fur rubbed
off and the pink in his ears turned gray, but the Boy
didn't notice; he thought the Rabbit was beautiful.
When summer came, they played together in the
woods almost every day.

Then one day the Boy got very sick. The doctor said that all the toys in the room had to go because they were full of germs. The Boy got better, but the little Rabbit was put in a sack with other things and taken outside.

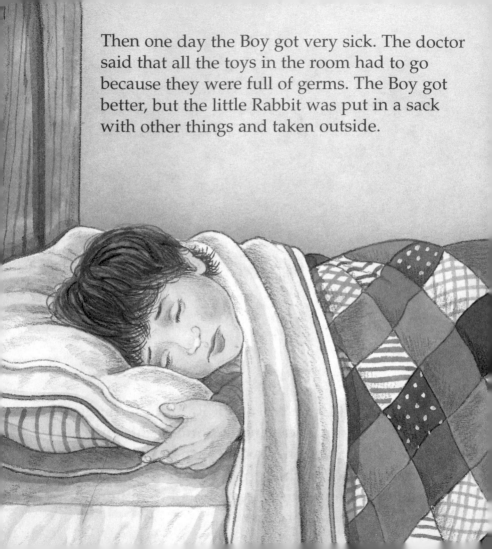

The Velveteen Rabbit wriggled his way to the top of the sack and looked out. Nearby he could see the woods where he and the Boy had played. He thought of how happy those times had been, and of how much the Boy had loved him. A tear trickled down his little shabby nose and fell to the ground.

Then a strange thing happened. Where the tear fell, a mysterious flower began to grow. It had emerald leaves and a beautiful golden blossom. The blossom opened and a fairy stepped out. "I am the toy magic Fairy," she said. "I take care of the playthings that children have loved. When they are old and worn out, I make them REAL."

"But wasn't I Real before?" the Rabbit asked. The fairy said, "You were Real to the Boy because he loved you. Now you shall be Real to everyone."

In the meadow the Velveteen Rabbit saw wild rabbits dancing with their shadows on the velvet grass. "Run and play, little Rabbit," said the fairy. "You are a Real Rabbit now."

Fall and winter passed; in the spring, when the days grew warm and sunny, the Boy went out to play. In the woods he saw two rabbits peeping at him from under a bush. One was grey, and the other had strange markings under his fur, as though he had once been spotted. His little soft nose and bright round eyes seemed familiar to the Boy.

"Why, that looks like my old bunny who got lost when I was sick," the Boy thought. He never knew that it really was his own Bunny, come back to look at the child who had first helped him to be Real.

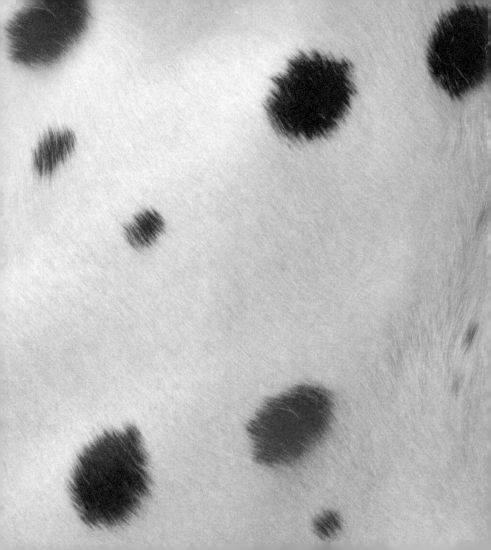